Something Like Murder

(Book Two — Secrets of the Deadwood)

Ashley Brandt

First published in 2023 by Blossom Spring Publishing
Something Like Murder (Secrets of the Deadwood Series)

ISBN 978-1-7395186-1-5
E: admin@blossomspringpublishing.com
W: www.blossomspringpublishing.com

Dedication:

To Sonnie, who has supported me from the first book, and Art, who has read them all. And to my cat, Peanut, the inspiration for Da Vinci.

Something Like Murder

Eddie smiled back at me like a cat who had cornered a mouse. His wide-toothed grin spread across his face, braces gleaming under the bright overhead lighting. His pale gray eyes were narrowed, and his face smattered with freckles. At sixteen, Eddie looked like the kid next door.

I ran my fingers over the yearbook page, recalling all the names and faces pictured there. I'd been out of high school for a decade, but some days, it seemed like longer than that. Sweet Scentsations, the candle store where I worked, was closed for renovations, so I'd opted to spend the extra time purging my closets. Da Vinci raised his head and yawned, stretching out his paws and arching his back. He'd spent the afternoon napping on the pillow beside the box that contained my high school days.

"Dunkridge?"

I looked up from my ruminations to Da Vinci's incredulous stare.

"What did you say?"

"I didn't know Eddie's last name was Dunkridge," Da Vinci said.

I shrugged and turned the page. I'd joined every club I could think of in my high school days, desperate to stay away from my mom and her drunken husband, Rick.

"Yes. Why does it matter?"

"The Dunkridges own that monstrosity over on Elm Lane," Da Vinci informed me.

Da Vinci was the feline equivalent of the town busybody; he knew of all the happenings in Corinth, though the only person he could tell was me. I'd adopted him from the animal shelter two summers ago at an adoption event. Though I'd intended to adopt a kitten, Da Vinci and I had formed a personal connection I couldn't deny, and I'd taken him home with me that day. Like me, Da Vinci was telepathic; but our skills were limited to each other.

"I believe they do," I confirmed patiently. "But what is the relevance?"

Da Vinci licked his paws and rolled his eyes at me.

"It's *not*, human. Except that they also own that nitwit of a mutt they call Sebastian. He's a Doberman, I think. I've had *fleas* more intelligent than he is."

"Ah."

Like most cats, Da Vinci hated dogs. I wasn't sure

what the Doberman had done to earn his ire, but clearly there was bad blood between the two. My cat held grudges.

"Look at that," he said, pausing his bath.

I followed his gaze to the living room window, which stood open to the immaculate front yard. I'd spent the last three days outside pruning the roses and pulling weeds. A fresh coat of river rock lined the pathway, and a new wind chime tinkled in the spring breeze. Martha Hattburg traipsed up the path, admiring my handiwork. Martha was a gardener herself — a fellow practitioner, I thought smugly.

"Good morning, Denali," Martha sang.

Clad in burgundy blouse and navy slacks, Martha looked ready for a day at the office. She had retired from her job at the car dealership in Frederickson two years ago, but dressed like she still worked there.

"Good morning, Martha. Come in."

Martha settled into one of the old kitchen chairs while I poured us each a mug of coffee. I didn't have visitors often, but Martha had been a good friend of my aunt Roni's, and by extension, me.

"The house looks nice," she complimented.

I thanked her and sipped the hot liquid, allowing it to burn all the way down. Martha's gaze assessed my curtains and the new paint job I'd completed over the winter. The trim was crisp white, and the walls a lovely robin's egg blue. The colors complimented my furniture well.

"I see Da Vinci has been eating well," she teased.

Da Vinci paused and glared up at my visitor, cursing her out in his brain. I was the only one to hear.

"Yes, he doesn't miss any meals," I added soberly.

I'm not the one who keeps an entire sleeve of cookies in my nightstand, Da Vinci retorted.

"Strictly medicinal," I murmured, much to Martha's confusion.

"Excuse me, dear?"

"Nothing."

"Have you heard about the Mendsters?"

I blinked at Martha. The name rang a bell, but it was difficult putting a face to the name. I shook my head.

"Oh, it was awful. Mrs. Mendster was found dead in her garden and her husband, Grant, was found hanging in the workshop behind the house!"

Da Vinci had stopped licking himself to listen intently.

My stomach lurched at the prospect of another murder here in Corinth, and so close to the Deadwoods.

"The Mendsters… they live out there by the woods, don't they?" I asked.

Martha sipped her coffee and winced. I'd forgotten she preferred cream in hers.

"Yes, they did, God rest their souls. Right on the edge of the Deadwoods. Word is that the land used to be a part of the woods themselves, but Grant's great grandfather purchased the last two acres a hundred years ago and used the cleared lumber to build himself a house. Grant Mendster added a workshop eight years ago for his projects.

Interesting, Da Vinci mused.

Very interesting, I agreed.

"Did you say Mr. Mendster hung himself? And they suspect he killed Mrs. Mendster?"

Martha's eyes widened.

"Oh no, dear! Grant worshipped the ground she walked on! The police are saying it was a third party."

Da Vinci and I exchanged looks.

"Do they have a suspect in mind?"

Last year, Sheriff Eagan had all but accused me of the

murder of the local realtor, Dan Cumberland. Cumberland had been after me to sell the house I'd inherited from my great aunt Roni, a proposition I'd adamantly refused. I'd been among the last to see Cumberland alive, and the first to discover his corpse. Not counting Da Vinci, of course.

"Not yet. But they're looking closely at that Plummer boy from Ralphsboro. Alex, I think his name is."

Da Vinci and I had heard of the man — a transplant from Mississippi, and some distant cousin to Ruth Johnson-Taylor, Martha's closest neighbor.

"We've heard of him!" I said, before realizing my faux pas.

Da Vinci gave me a scathing look and Martha stared between us, confused.

"You've um…"

"I've heard of the man," I corrected calmly. "He's from Mississippi, isn't he?"

"Yes, he is," she said crisply (Martha didn't hold Mississippians in high regard).

"Why do you suspect him?"

She looked at me like the answer was obvious.

"The timing is rather convenient," she said. "This

sullen young man arrives and two months later our oldest residents turn up dead! And just three days before, he'd gone over there looking for work. The rumor is this Alex fella has a sordid past and a reputation that followed him," she added primly. "Mr. Mendster knew about it and told that young man to get lost! They had words, the way I hear it, and Alex Plummer promised Grant Mendster he'd regret the decision. The following night, the back acre of their property caught fire; no one can say how it started."

Martha raised an eyebrow and nodded, then glanced at the wall clock and rose.

"I'm afraid this is where I leave you," Martha pronounced. "I've got errands to run."

Thank Bob, Da Vinci thought dryly.

I walked Martha out and closed the door behind her. Da Vinci glared at me from his spot on the pillow.

"That old bat needs to find something to do other than gossip," he said.

"I wonder about the murders," I told him. "That's two more within the year — all of which occurred in the Deadwoods."

Da Vinci resumed his bath.

"There are ghosts there," he said offhandedly.

I arched my brows and carried the empty coffee mugs to the sink to wash.

"In the Deadwoods?"

"Mhmm."

"Why do you say so?"

Da Vinci pulled his paw over his ear and shook his head.

"I've heard them at night. They inhabit the trees, I think. Tomlin's cat says the Deadwoods are an old burial ground of some kind. The trees represent the souls of the corpses planted there. If the Mendsters were foolish enough to cut down those trees and use them to build houses, it's no wonder they were murdered. The dead don't take kindly to desecration."

I watched the cat resume his routine, marveling at the new insight. Da Vinci had always been a levelheaded feline, more so than most humans. His proclamation of ghosts and haunted houses had come as a surprise.

"You don't think it's the interloper?" I asked.

Da Vinci shrugged.

"Could be. But I'd bet tuna it's the ghosts."

"I need to meet this Plummer fella," I said.

Alex Plummer was right where Ruth Johnson-Taylor said he would be. At a far table in the Corinth public library, Alex was not what I had envisioned when Da Vinci and I had hatched our plan. After a little brainstorming, Da Vinci decided the best way to meet the self-proclaimed handyman was to break something, a task Da Vinci relished. We'd debated back and forth before I agreed to let the cat scratch up the doorway leading to the tiny bathroom off the hall. I'd intended to paint the trim anyway, and it gave me an excuse to hire this Plummer man. Da Vinci relished the task.

I hesitated behind a tall shelf of self-help books, watching the man engrossed in his book. Alex was tall and well-built, with strong arms and a lean body. His hair was dark and trimmed close to his head, and his skin a lovely golden color, painted by the sun. Tattoos snaked up his arms, complex and bold, like the man, I thought. I almost choked when he looked up and scanned around him, fixing me in his dark gaze. Gasping, I retreated in haste, bumping into the book cart left behind me and falling sideways.

In a desperate attempt to break my fall, I reached out, bumping a stack of books being re-catalogued and bringing them down with me. The metal cart crashed behind me, knocking a dozen more books loose on top of my prone body. I considered lying still in the aisle, feigning death. I could hear the concerned whispers of the other patrons and the footfalls of people coming to investigate. I squeezed my eyes shut tight, willing the carpet to swallow me whole.

I risked a glance up, and my eyes landed on a pair of black work boots. I traced them up the long legs and further still, past the black T-shirt and the familiar arms. That same pair of eyes stared down at me, and Alex Plummer reached down to brush his fingers along my neck.

"Well, you're not dead," he said pragmatically.

"I kind of wish I was," I admitted.

He cracked a small smile and waved the rest of the patrons away, hauling me up from the pile of books.

"What happened?"

My heart thrummed in my chest as I cast around for a reasonable explanation. I could tell him I'd tripped while spying, or I could make up an excuse.

"Low blood sugar," I stammered.

"You're diabetic?"

Alex studied me beneath furrowed brows, the concern marking his gorgeous features.

"No. Just got a little dizzy while I was browsing the books," I rallied.

Hastily, I grabbed the closest title from the shelf without reading it.

"*The Newcomer's Guide to Sexual Dysfunction*," he read.

I squeaked and tossed the book aside. The hole I was digging just got deeper and deeper.

"Not that one," I stammered. "I don't have — I mean I don't need…"

"Forget it. Why don't we get you some food to get that blood sugar back up? My best friend back home has diabetes and it's no joke. Come on, there's a bakery next door."

Before I could protest, Alex Plummer had hold of my hand and was leading me out of the library and into the Seracuse Family Bakery.

The smell of dark roast and sticky buns permeated the air of the little café. Alex and I sat opposite each other in one of the back booths, coffees in hand. I'd polished off two sticky buns at Alex's insistence, conscious of the way he watched me like the cat watching the canary. The café was quaint, decorated in browns and blues and accented in florals. It was one of my favorite places to frequent, along with the library.

"You're new in town?"

Alex gulped down his coffee and leaned back in the booth.

"I'm from Mississippi. I'm renting a room at my cousin's house for the time being. Have you met Ruth Taylor?"

"I've known Ruth for years. She and my great aunt Roni were close, once upon a time."

Alex nodded.

"I hear you do handiwork," I said, finishing my coffee.

"I do a little."

"As it happens, I've got a little project I need done.

My cat, Da Vinci, has developed a scratching problem and has gouged the bathroom door jamb. I thought rather than filling it with spackle, I'd just have the thing replaced, instead."

"I could handle that."

"Good. Can you start tomorrow?"

Alex stared out the window and drummed his fingers on the table.

"Sure. I've got to finish up some electrical work this afternoon, but tomorrow I'm free."

"Perfect. Uh — what do you charge?"

"I don't guess the job will cost more than fifty dollars. Jambs are cheap and easy to replace if you've got the tools to do it."

"Perfect. I uh — I can pick you up if that suits you?"

"Don't go to the trouble. I know where you live."

His statement both alarmed and excited me. Wait until I told Da Vinci.

Alex arrived on time the following morning. Da Vinci

perched on the countertop, regarding the man with a shrewd stare. I'd told that cat dozens of times that he wasn't allowed on the counter, but Da Vinci was a tough nut to crack.

"Get off the counter," I warned him quietly.

He nodded at me and made his way to the appointed door jamb to assess the damage.

"Make me," Da Vinci hissed.

"I can have this jamb replaced in a few hours," Alex announced. "I've got to make a trip to the home repair store downtown for the parts, but I can get it done today."

After a little more discussion, Alex left, leaving Da Vinci and I alone again.

"He's not a murderer," Da Vinci announced.

I didn't think so, either.

"Oh? Are you psychic now, too, Da Vinci?"

"I happen to be an excellent judge of character. I picked *you*, didn't I?"

Da Vinci's backhanded compliment had caught me off guard.

"*I* picked *you*," I corrected him.

"I don't think the Plummer man killed anyone."

"I don't, either. But who did?"

That night, Da Vinci kept me awake until well past midnight with his musings. His voice filled my head with ramblings about the new cat in town — a brown tabby from some big city on the east coast. The thing about city cats, he said, was that they were either mannerless wretches or completely domesticated. Da Vinci fancied himself superior in that regard.

"You like her," I offered, smiling into the dark.

Da Vinci huffed.

"And you have the hots for that Plummer man from Mississippi," he chided.

"Maybe so," I grinned.

"He's from *Mississippi*," Da Vinci reiterated.

"And you're from the Corinth County animal shelter," I reminded him.

"Anyway, in case you were listening, her name is Cloe, and her humans moved here from New Jersey. Maybe one of *them* killed the Mendsters."

"You're confident the killers are out-of-towners?"

Da Vinci used his paw to clean his face, making wet,

sloppy noises in the otherwise quiet bedroom.

"Perhaps not. It could be that whoever murdered the pair also killed that realtor and your boyfriend at the coroner's office."

"Eddie was *not* my boyfriend," I reminded him.

Da Vinci grumbled and leapt off the bed, sauntering out into the kitchen to drink from the faucet. After that I lay awake, alone under the covers, lost in my own musings of Alex Plummer and the Mendster murders.

The next morning, Da Vinci and I sat agape while the news anchor for *Corinth Daily News* interviewed the pastor of the little Baptist church three blocks from my house. Pastor Donovan wore a pressed suit for the occasion, with a somber gray tie and his thinning hair combed carefully into place. Though the rest of him was unremarkable, Pastor Donovan had striking grey eyes and unusually sharp teeth.

"One of my sheep delivered the news this morning," Donovan said regrettably. "It's tragic, Janine. First two of our most respected citizens are found murdered on their own property, and then one of our newest guests, Alex Plummer, goes missing overnight. I'm afraid our little town just isn't what it used to be."

The Pastor leveled a meaningful gaze at the reporter. Janine, whose blonde hair was twisted and sprayed to perfection, nodded in agreement.

"Terrible news, Pastor. Thank you for speaking with us."

"Anytime, Ms. Addams. See you Sunday," he added with a congenial wink.

A flustered Janine resumed her narrative while the cameraman panned in and out of the town's inner streets, homing in on the library and the café Alex and I visited yesterday.

"Holy salmon skins," Da Vinci breathed. "Isn't that the café you and what's-his-name went for coffee?"

"It is. And apparently 'what's his name' has vanished," I said.

I didn't like how close to home this entire debacle had become. A murder itself was unsettling, especially in a small town like Corinth; chances were, you knew the killer — sat next to them in church or stood behind them in the grocery line. Worse yet, the man under suspicion had vanished overnight, without leaving word. Could it be he'd fallen prey to whoever was killing the citizens in Corinth? Or had he run off to evade authorities?

"You know what I think," Da Vinci began.

"No, but I'm sure I'm about to find out."

He ignored the comment.

"I think we should go down there to Ruth's place and poke around her cousin's room, see if we turn up anything. Maybe that little tabby from Jersey will be out and about," he purred.

"She lives nearby?"

Da Vinci had omitted that part of the story.

"Yes, about a quarter mile down the road from Ruth's place," he said, licking his tail.

That made two newcomers and two murders. And a missing suspect.

Ruth Johnson-Taylor was an emotional mess. True to southern etiquette, her dining room table was littered with ready-to-eat meals, casseroles, and baked goods delivered by the neighbors. No one knew for sure what had happened to Alex Plummer, but considering the recent murders, it didn't look good for Ruth.

"Did he say anything before he vanished?" I pressed her carefully.

Ruth sniffed and blew into a handkerchief stitched with blue thread.

"No. In fact, he came home happier than usual and asked to have pecan pie for dessert today. Denali, he wouldn't have just left, like this! Something awful must have happened to him, and the police are looking at him as a suspect and not as a victim."

I couldn't say that I knew Alex well, but I was a good judge of character. And, despite his cantankerous disposition, so was Da Vinci. Neither of us believed him capable of committing murder. I did wonder about the new neighbors, the ones Da Vinci had informed of just this morning.

"That was kind of your neighbors," I told Ruth, pointing to the casserole dishes on the table.

"Yes. Darling," she agreed.

"Speaking of neighbors, I heard you have new ones?"

“I have,” she confirmed. “Mr. Evan Pratt and his teenaged son, Will. They’re transplants from New Jersey, I think.”

“I wonder how they managed to find Corinth,” I mused.

“Mr. Pratt’s a widower,” she whispered. “His son got involved in some bad happenings back in the city, and Mr. Evans thought it prudent to relocate somewhere close-knit and quiet.”

I shot a meaningful look at Da Vinci, who was occupied with Ruth’s laundry hamper. He stuck his nose into one of the gaps in the side, recoiling with disgust.

Good giblets, woman, don’t you bathe?

Focus, Da Vinci.

Come and smell this dirty stocking, first, and then tell me to focus, he retorted.

I bent to retrieve Da Vinci, who yowled in protest. I felt my heart skip a beat when my eyes drifted across a wrinkled blouse, stuffed down in the center of the hamper, along with the soiled stockings Da Vinci had smelled. The stockings looked as though Ruth had been trudging through muddy water; they were caked in mud. The blouse, on the other hand, had a torn seam on the shoulder. And droplets of blood.

"I suppose we'd better head home," I announced with false cheer.

I hoped Ruth hadn't seen me inspecting her hamper. She didn't appear suspicious; she was lifting the foil cover of one of the casserole dishes on the counter.

"Alright dear, thanks for stopping by."

Do you see what I mean? Da Vinci thought, as I carried him briskly away from Ruth's house.

Did you see the blood? I thought.

The bedroom was dark and silent. Da Vinci snored softly on the pillow beside me, his body curled inward, and his face turned upward. The night was clear and cool, with the occasional wind gust. The bedside clock read midnight, and I wondered why I had started awake so suddenly. The hairs on the back of my neck stood on end, and a chill shot down through my spine. Da Vinci perked his head up, having detected the source of my unease.

Someone's in the house, he thought to me.

Nodding silently, I slipped out of the bed covers and crept toward the closet to my right. I didn't have any weapons, but I did keep an old golf club stowed behind my winter coat, for instances like these. I'd never had occasion to use it, thank goodness, but it appeared my luck had run out.

Can you tell who? I thought to the cat.

No. His footsteps are heavy. Long strides. It's a man, I think.

I eyed the phone on the opposite side of the bedroom, wishing for all I was worth I could get to it in time. Crossing the room meant crossing the doorway, and the intruder lurked just outside of it and down the hallway.

Steady. Steady… Da Vinci whispered.

With a fierce yowl, Da Vinci sprung toward the attacker, ambushing him in the doorway. The man yelped and stumbled back, his hands searching for the source of his pain. Da Vinci was fierce, his claws digging into the man's scalp, his plump little body scurrying from shoulder to shoulder and back up again. Gripping the handle, I swung the golf club, hitting the man in his stomach. With a great, "oof!", he doubled over, and Da Vinci leapt down to stand beside me.

"Wait! Don't hit me!"

My stomach flipped a second time when I recognized the man's voice. I switched on the bedside lamp and peered down at a bedraggled Alex Plummer, his shirt torn and his face bleeding. He hunched over on his knees, guarding his abdomen with his right arm and extending the left up in a pleading gesture.

I rallied.

"What the devil are you doing in my house?!" I shouted.

Alex gasped, and tears streaked down his rugged face.

"I'm sorry. I couldn't let anyone know I was in town. I — I need your help."

Alex groaned as he swallowed the pain reliever tablets I'd given him. He perched on my great aunt's antique armchair, which I made a mental note to have recovered.

"Talk," Da Vinci said.

Startled, I looked down at the cat, trying to think of a way to excuse a talking feline. The ghostly pale color of

Alex's face was almost humorous, under different circumstances.

"Did your cat just talk to me?"

Da Vinci flicked his tail in annoyance. Leaping up onto the armchair, he circled around Alex's head like shark hunting prey.

"I can do a lot more than just talk, buddy boy," my cat threatened, "so I suggest you explain to me why you opted to wake me out of a delightful sleep instead of knocking on the door like most humans do."

Alex darted a gaze at me, and I nodded toward the cat, as if to say, *don't look at me.*

I had to give the Plummer man due credit; he recovered quickly.

"A few days before that old couple got murdered, I'd gone out that way looking for work. Someone referred me to the Mendster place, saying they needed help digging a well on their property. Only when I got there, Mr. Mendster intercepted me at the gates, hurling accusations at me and threatening me if I ever stepped foot on his property again."

Alex paused to survey our matching expressions.

"Go on," I prompted.

I stood with my arms crossed, body leaning against the opposite wall. I'd propped the golf club next to me, and Da Vinci sat a hairsbreadth from the intruder's head. Waiting.

"I left. The next day I heard talk they'd been found dead. That Mr. Mendster didn't seem right in the head, so I assumed he'd killed his wife and then hung himself. But the police are convinced someone else perpetrated the crime. Since I was the new guy in town and had words with Mr. Mendster the day before his death, that sheriff zeroed in on me like a hawk on a mouse.

I think he's telling the truth, I thought to Da Vinci.

I suppose he is.

"I just figured I'd lay low and wait out the investigation until that new family living down the road from my great aunt's house cornered me on my way back home from the coffee shop the other night. The man — Evan Pratt, is a mean son-of-a-gun, and his son isn't much better. Both were carrying pistols and had a wolfdog with them, and both were spitting angry. Evan Pratt seemed to think I'd committed those murders, and he threatened me. He said he and that boy of his had come to Corinth for a clean slate, and neither needed the attention of the law. They blamed me, told me to leave town. They said if I didn't, my cousin Ruth could end up just like the Mendsters. Or the other two before them."

I could feel Da Vinci's shock as clearly as I could feel my own. How was it that the Pratts knew about the other murders? I supposed it was possible they'd heard the gossip or seen it in past news articles. Come to think of it, the recent coverage of the Mendsters' deaths had mentioned it once or twice, in passing.

"What can I do for you that the sheriff can't?" I asked Alex.

"You can believe me, for starters."

Da Vinci issued a warning growl, and Alex flinched.

"I suppose if you can believe in my talking cat, I can believe in your innocence. For now, at least," I said.

"Housemate," Da Vinci corrected acidly.

"Excuse me. My talking *housemate*."

The three of us stayed up long into the early morning hours. I'd told Alex about his cousin's blouse, though not without reservations. To my surprise, Alex hardly flinched when I delivered the news.

"I suppose I should tell you the real reason I ran," he admitted morosely. "I started to suspect Cousin Ruth."

"And you're just telling us this now?!" Da Vinci chided.

"I'm sorry! Look, Ruth is family. I haven't seen her in years, but we share blood. I couldn't just accuse her of something like murder! I had to get to the bottom of this, first. Will you help me?"

"I'll check with my sources," Da Vinci said smugly.

Though my housemate resented being woken from his nighttime sleep, I knew he basked in the glow of new information, intrigue, and the chance to be right.

"I think you and I have to get inside Ruth's house and get a better look at those soiled clothes," I told Alex.

The following night, Alex and I crept along the perimeter of Ruth's place. Heavy fog had rolled in from the north, providing us with added cover; paired with the call of the night owl and the rustle of moving things nearby, the creepy factor skyrocketed, and I considered turning back more than once. But I knew Alex's freedom depended on the answers we could find in his cousin's house; and Corinth needed its murderer caught.

Slipping past the living room windows, Alex led the way toward the back door, which Ruth forgot to lock on occasion. The back door led to her little vegetable garden, which was in the beginning phase of growth. Piles of sand lined the moist bed in rows, overwatered the day before. A trowel, a bucket, and assorted hand tools lined the wall of the house, and a trio of small, wooden steps led up to the back door. Which, as Alex had anticipated, was unlocked.

He slipped inside first, with me close at his heels. I felt like the lowest type of human, skulking around someone else's house at night. Alex moved swiftly and silently, and with more confidence than I cared to examine.

"In here," he whispered, tugging me along.

I tried to ignore the way his cool fingers sent chills up my arm, and the way my heart hammered with excitement. Passing through the parlor, we reached the laundry area off the kitchen, where I'd seen the soiled clothing in the hamper a day before. Only the hamper was empty.

I gasped when the kitchen light flicked on.

Alex spun to face his cousin, who stood opposite us, with a rifle pointed at us both.

"I thought you'd show up here again," she told Alex. "Looking for something, cousin?"

"I didn't mean to frighten you, Ruth. I… uh… I'd forgotten some of my things and I…"

Ruth took a step forward and aimed the rifle higher.

"Enough with your lies!"

Shifting her gaze at me, a malevolent smile spread across her lips.

"Did he tell you about our retirement plan, Denali?"

I glanced from Ruth to Alex, perplexed. Judging by my accomplice's morose expression, he knew she was about to reveal something unpleasant.

"We used to rob banks," she told me.

"*You* robbed banks! I wanted no part of it!" protested Alex.

"Stop your sniveling, Alex. You drove the getaway car. You're just as culpable!"

"Alex," I breathed.

"Please, Denali… it's not what you're thinking…"

Ruth tossed her head back and cackled. Suddenly the friendly older woman I'd known for most of my life had taken on a new persona. Even finding the soiled clothes, I'd discounted it until now. The Ruth I'd known couldn't have committed such an egregious crime. But *this* Ruth could.

"Alex's daddy needed a hand up," Ruth told me. "He'd gotten in debt with some very bad people, hadn't he, Alex? That was when we decided to go into the bank robbing business together. I did all the heavy lifting, of course. Alex was hardly driving age at that time. We robbed ten banks up and down the east coast and two on the way here!" she laughed again.

"I gave it up," Alex defended.

"Oh yes, you gave it up, just like I gave it up. But the apple never falls far from the tree, does it, cousin?"

Forgetting the gun, Alex turned to face me.

"Denali, my dad got into trouble again. He's got stage three cancer and a gambling addiction. I couldn't let them kill him. I got in, too, just to buy his way out of trouble. Only the dealer was dirty, and we lost everything. They killed him before we got out." Alex said.

Rage and pity warred inside of me. This man had lied to me more than once about who he was and what he was doing. But if Ruth's story was true, did I blame him for protecting his dad? To what extent would I have gone to protect the ones I loved?

All the way, Da Vinci's voice answered my brain. Then, a second realization hit me, just as jarring and painful as the first.

"You killed the Mendsters because they knew who you were?"

I felt like the air had been knocked out of my chest.

"No! I swear it, Denali, I'm not a murderer!"

"He's telling the truth, dear," Ruth interjected. "*I* am."

The rifle went off with a deafening blast just as Alex dove into me, knocking me sideways. I cried out as my head hit the wall, sending shooting pain through my skull. I scrambled up, trying to focus my eyes through blurred vision. Alex was grappling with Ruth, the rifle lying to their right. I'd never held a gun before, but I needed to get my hands on that rifle.

"Denali!"

Da Vinci's harried voice shouted at me from across the way. I tried to see straight, but my cat danced and contorted into doubles in my vision.

"Da Vinci? When did you get here?" I asked dazed.

Ruth paused her struggle, eyes darting from me to the animal.

"That bloody cat can *talk*?!" she screeched.

With a dizzying speed, Da Vinci nosed the gun toward me, and I dove for it, narrowly missing Ruth's savage hands as she dove for it. Alex wrestled with his cousin while I grabbed the gun and aimed it. Before I could issue my warning, Ruth scrambled up and charged me, and I fired. Alex watched in horror as his cousin-turned-murderess stumbled back into his arms before sliding to the floor. The shotgun blast had left its terrible mark on her chest, blood blossoming on her night dress. Ruth would expire before anyone arrived to help.

"The cat can *talk*," she reiterated.

And then she died.

What had begun as a late excursion night had evolved into a very long day. Alex and I were rigorously interviewed by the press; including questions we'd been warned by the sheriff not to answer. As far as the police were concerned, the Mendster murders was an ongoing investigation. Sheriff Eagan couldn't solve the case by my word alone. Or Alex's.

Da Vinci returned home, after ensuring my safety. Ruth Johnson-Taylor, aka the Mendster murderer, lay dead on her kitchen floor, her body covered with a sheet. Alex told the police the same thing he'd told his cousin when she'd discovered us skulking around in her kitchen: he'd returned to pick up a few of the personal items Ruth had agreed to store in her home. She'd given him a key, so it wasn't breaking and entering. To explain my involvement, Alex told the police we were dating, and that I'd been trying to convince him to remain in town.

Alex related the threat from the Pratts, but I wasn't sure the sheriff would allocate many resources to the issue. With two recent murders and two older ones, Corinth law enforcement had its hands full. The police dismissed us sometime after noon, and Alex and I dragged ourselves back to my house, where Da Vinci waited on the sofa. While Alex and I took turns using the shower, my cat retold the confrontation with Ruth, and his acts of heroism. I dished his tuna while I listened to him explain that it was the Pratts' cat who had clued him in on their closest neighbor.

"She told me that the day the Mendsters were killed, Ruth came home coated in blood, a length of rope draped around her shoulder. She was muttering like a mad woman, according to Chloe."

I hadn't told Da Vinci about Chloe's owners; I'd save that for another time.

Days later, it came to light that Ruth Johnson-Taylor had paid a visit to Mrs. Mendster (a routine, according to their common acquaintances), and killed her in the garden. The murder weapon, they said, had been a pair of nearby gardening shears.

Then, feigning surprise, Ruth screamed for Mr. Mendster, claiming his wife had had a terrible accident. While Gary Mendster tended to his wife, Ruth struck him over the head with the shovel, using a length of rope and her old pickup to drag him over to his workshop, where she staged the rest. The Mendsters had heard through the grapevine that Alex had a past, but no one thought to question Ruth herself. Nevertheless, Ruth took no chances.

With Da Vinci engrossed in his bowl of tuna, Alex and I settled into the sofa, glued to the evening news. Da Vinci took credit for solving the Mendster murders; an assertion I didn't contest. Sheriff Eagan told the public it was the department who had cracked the case, with no mention of Alex and me. I supposed it was better, that way. As for the murders preceding it, those remained a mystery.

Deadwoods Book 3 Teaser

All That Remains

I held the fourth tissue to my nose and blew. My eyes leaked like the plumbing in the women's restroom at Seracuse Family Bakery downtown, and I knew without looking that my nose was red and swollen from congestion. Da Vinci perched beside me on our overstuffed brown sofa, his face turned up in a mixture of disgust and confusion.

"I'll never understand why you humans get so sentimental over a television show," he told me.

I blew my nose again, discarding the used tissue in the wastebasket near my feet.

"It's a *movie*," I argued, "and it's a classic."

Da Vinci groaned.

"And you call yourselves the superior species," he grumbled. "This entire problem could've been mitigated with a bit of communication. Or patience," he added.

I refrained from commenting on *his* patience, which was lacking.

"That's the point of it," I explained. "They're star-crossed lovers. Their families would've never allowed them to be together, and they knew it."

I started sobbing again, earning another groan from my housemate.

"I can't stand it any longer," he told me at last. "I'm going to go chase mice."

I nodded as Da Vinci sauntered across the living room and heaved his generous body out the large pet door Alex had installed three months earlier. It was designed with dogs in mind, but Da Vinci required larger accommodations.

Thinking of Alex triggered another onslaught of tears. Alex Plummer and I had dated since we'd solved the Mendster murders two years earlier. The closer I crept to thirty, the more impatient I became, at least in secret. Though I preferred to live life by the minute, I had hopes for a family of my own, and as time leached away, my hopes dwindled. I decided that a romantic tragedy was the worst decision I'd made in movie selections, at least this soon after a breakup.

Turning off the television set, I gathered myself and replaced the wastebasket to its rightful spot underneath the antique desk on the opposite wall. I left the box of tissues on the counter and washed my hands, splashing a little cold water on my tear-stained cheeks.

I'd convinced myself that Alex had plans to propose. That was why, on the evening he sat us down to talk three weeks ago, my heart was fluttering like a hummingbird's wings. And why, when he'd explained he was moving back to Mississippi instead, my dreams of becoming Mrs. Plummer shattered.

"Moving?!" I cried.

Alex had the grace to look somber, though I wondered how genuine it was.

"My dad's sister is in hospice care," he'd explained. "With dad gone, she's got no one else."

For a fleeting moment, I'd considered offering to move with him — but the reality sunk in that he hadn't asked me to.

"But — what about us? I mean — are you coming back to Corinth?"

Alex drummed his fingers on the tabletop and glanced all around. Seracuse Family Bakery was alive with the sounds of happiness and the smells of freshly brewed caffeine. On any normal day, I'd indulge in one of their cinnamon tarts and a side of black coffee. Today, not even my favorite pastry sounded appealing. I felt cold and empty.

"I don't think so, Denali," he admitted.

I'd gotten up and left after that; any remaining questions I might've posed answered in a single sentence. If I'd stayed, I could've asked them anyway, and cried for my own benefit — but I'd gathered what remained of my pride and walked away, the word *goodbye* dying on my lips. I'd never been very good at goodbyes.

Where had we gone wrong, I wondered? Alex and I had had a wonderful relationship — at least I'd thought so. His departure had come out of right field, and in the deepest parts of my heart, I wondered if his dealings with the nasty characters back home were truly extinct. It was Da Vinci who had recommended I do the internet search and investigate my ex-boyfriend's past. In less than an hour, I'd uncovered the truth.

"A fiancée," I sobbed.

I stood over the kitchen sink, staring absently out the window and into the thriving garden. To combat my depression, I'd spent countless hours knee-deep in soil, scraping and digging and planting the tears away. If my aunt Roni could see it, she'd be impressed. I ached a little more for her now, as I craved the loving arms of comfort and understanding. Instead, I had Da Vinci, who detested human emotions, and was about as cuddly as a porcupine.

According to internet records, Alex Plummer had left behind a fiancée — a lovely blonde with ice-blue eyes and the skin of an angel. I hated her already. I'd left a nasty voicemail on his answering machine, which he'd returned the following day. He'd claimed they'd broken up before he'd left Mississippi and got in touch again a few months before his return. With his aunt's failing health and his ex-fiancée urging him to reconcile, Alex's former life beckoned him, and he'd answered the call.

"No more men," I swore to the ceramic bird on my windowsill. Then, feeling empowered, I gathered all the cleaning solutions underneath the sink and started cleaning. I'd scrub every bit of that man off my furniture and out of my life. And I did.

For the next two weeks, my house remained immaculate. I'd taken extra care with my outward appearance, too —

adding an extra few cosmetics to my regimen and a delightful body spray I found on sale at Sweet Scentsations, the candle shop where I'd worked for the last seven years. I decided that if I was going to become an old spinster, I'd at least make a good looking one. After all, who said spinsters had to be ugly?

Da Vinci napped at home as I crossed Macon Blvd. toward the empty lot that abutted my house. That lot had once been home to an antiques dealer, but the shop owners had gone into foreclosure, leaving the place to deteriorate. Several years later, the city came in and demolished the shop, leaving behind a vacant plot that never sold.

I started at the movement in my peripheral. Pedestrians cut through this lot all the time, but none had been around when I'd crossed the road. I paused mid-step as a tall man stood up from his kneeling position about twenty yards to my left. He was tanned and lean, with sandy blond hair and dark eyes. I estimated him to be in his mid-forties.

"Hi," I said uneasily.

I knew most of the inhabitants of Corinth, but I'd never seen this man before.

The stranger glanced around us and then behind himself, confirming that my words were indeed directed at him.

"Hello," he said cautiously.

"I don't believe we've met," I said, closing the gap between us and extending my hand. "I'm Denali."

I arranged my face in what I hoped was a charming smile. The man accepted my handshake, his own grasp cold and dry.

"Rupert," he said.

Rupert had a vague European accent, making even his name sound elegant when spoken. Perhaps he was visiting someone in town? He looked lost.

"Are you looking for something?" I asked.

Rupert had crouched there in the dried grass inspecting something in the dirt.

"Oh — no, I thought I saw something peculiar. It turned out to be nothing," he said.

All of a sudden, I felt the distinct feeling of being watched. I scanned the perimeter of my house, catching sight of Da Vinci's plump form in my bedroom window.

Tuna! he mouthed.

I clutched the bags in my right hand and a fresh

bouquet of flowers in my left. I'd gone to the little grocery on the corner for tuna and bought myself some flowers on a whim. There was nothing like a fresh bouquet to brighten one's mood.

"If there's nothing I can do for you, I ought to get back home. I live over there," I told him, pointing to the little house. "It was lovely to meet you, Rupert," I finished uncomfortably.

Though I wasn't exactly embedded in Corinth's social circles, I wasn't a recluse by any means, and talking to people had never proven difficult before. With Rupert, I felt unsettled. Something about the newcomer triggered warning bells in my head. He was both foreign and familiar, and utterly out of place.

"It was a pleasure, Miss Denali," he said.

I turned to go, telling Da Vinci through thought to hold his horses. Then, reconsidering, I decided to invite Rupert for coffee, remembering southern etiquette. Since I was certain he would decline, there was no harm in making the gesture. Only when I turned around, the plot was vacant behind me, and Rupert had vanished. I scanned the roads in every direction, noting the familiar bodies that milled around town. The paper boy rode by on his bicycle, and a pair of stray dogs trotted down the avenue that intersected Macon Blvd. I peered further west toward the deadwoods, seeing no one. It was as if the newcomer had vanished into thin air.

Hungry! Da Vinci's voice shouted in my head.

So, I crossed the remaining stretch of land between my house and the grocery store and locked my front door behind me.

The next morning, I sat at the kitchen table with my feet propped on the other chair. My legs stuck out from my bathrobe, smooth and slightly golden from the sun. Summer had come early this year, and the time I'd spent gardening outdoors had done wonders for my skin. I waggled my toes, admiring the fuzzy pink slippers on my feet. The coffee tasted good, and the birds sang lightheartedly beyond the open windows. As a part of my post-breakup existence, I'd determined to pay closer attention to the pleasant things in life, rather than lamenting something I'd never had. While I didn't exactly wish Alex Plummer well, I didn't harbor any ill will.

Taking another sip of the coffee, I perused the local newspaper, scanning the section about Cold Case Anniversaries. Corinth was a small town, but even small towns had crime. The sheriff's department liked to feature certain cold cases in the news articles, hoping to glean new information. I nearly spat out the coffee when a familiar face stared blankly from the black and white pages, his eyes distant and focused on something I couldn't see.

A century after the disappearance of Rupert Vallance, the Corinth County undertaker, the sheriff's office is still seeking any information regarding his disappearance. Vallance was a model citizen and a family man, according to his neighbors and colleagues. Mr. Vallance had just been awarded the Certificate of Distinguished Performance after his contributions led to the solving of a triple murder case. Just two days after the award ceremony, Mr. Vallance failed to report to work, and his family stated that he'd left home three hours before. Police launched an extensive investigation, but due to budget and technological constraints, no conclusive evidence was ever recovered, and the case went cold.

The sheriff's department is asking anyone with any information to call the tip hotline printed below. Reporters will remain anonymous.

In other news, the Petrol Station on the corner of Juniper and Hanson Road went up in flames sometime last night. Arson investigators were called to the scene and investigations are under way..."

I drifted toward the television screen, muting the news reporter's narration. The photograph of the missing man was still pictured in the upper right corner of the screen. My stomach flipped when I recognized him as doppelganger to the one I'd spoken to only yesterday; according to the news story, his name was Rupert Vallance, and he'd gone missing a century ago. The article did say that Vallance had had a family; I supposed the Vallance genetics could be strong enough to yield an exact lookalike; perhaps the man I'd met yesterday was a descendant of the missing Mr. Vallance. Nevertheless, the likeness was unsettling.

"I've seen him," Da Vinci volunteered.

Leaping up onto the tabletop, Da Vinci's body rattled the cup and saucer I'd been drinking from. I hated it when he climbed on top of the furniture, but my mind was too busy piecing together the article to chide him for it.

"You've seen this man?" I questioned, showing him the picture.

"Mhmm," Da Vinci said, licking his front paws.

"Where?"

"The Deadwoods," he remarked.

I rolled my eyes.

"Very funny, Da Vinci," I said.

Though my housemate was pragmatic about most things, he had the ridiculous notion that the Deadwoods were home to ghosts. While I considered myself open-minded, I wasn't sold on the idea of the living dead.

"I'm serious. The best mice inhabit the Deadwood, especially at night. I've seen him there, ghosting around. He appeared to be searching for something."

I couldn't ignore the goosebumps that rippled down my arms.

"Did you two ever talk?"

Da Vinci paused his cleaning to study my face.

"I think I called him a nasty name," my housemate admitted. "He scared away the mice."

Da Vinci muttered something about a nap and jumped down, leaving me to muse about the missing man. It was impossible that the Rupert I'd met the day before was the same Rupert who had gone missing a hundred years ago. Wasn't it?

Acknowledgements

Huge thanks to my close friends and co-workers, who read the beginning books of this series and offered feedback. Many thanks to my publisher and everyone involved in the publishing process — your work is incredible. Finally, thanks to my friend Logan, who understands my humor, claps when I fall, and quotes the best comedies. Everyone should have a friend like you!

About the Author

Ashley Brandt is from Southern California. She lives in North Texas with her loving husband and two wonderful boys. Ashley has been reading and writing stories since she was very young, and enjoys spinning colorful tales with extraordinary characters. She has published four books and some poetry, and plans to publish future works.

Ashley attended junior college in Texas, earning her Degree in Applied Science and Paramedicine. Ashley works as a Licensed Paramedic in North Texas, and she is passionate about helping people. She has worked as a healthcare provider for over eight years, and serves as an adjunct instructor for the EMS program at the college she attended.

In her spare time, Ashley enjoys photography, swimming, hiking, and volunteers with the Big Brother/Big Sister Program. She fosters kittens for the local animal shelter and loves to garden. Ashley's passion for writing comes from a lifetime of immersive reading, and the desire to create a beautiful escape for her readers. In books, anything is possible! Ashley finds inspiration from the people and places she encounters and enjoys creating literary heroes from real-life ones.

www.ingramcontent.com/pod-product-compliance
Lightning Source LLC
LaVergne TN
LVHW040959150826
845672LV00002B/777